Richard Adam's

Watership Down

BookCaps™ Study Guide
<u>www.bookcaps.com</u>

© 2012. All Rights Reserved.

Table of Contents

Historical Context

Richard Adams was born in England in 1920 and has been working as an author full time since 1974. Before he began writing full time, he had been in the British Army and then worked as a civil servant. While he was working as a civil servant, he wrote "Watership Down," which is widely known as Adams' most successful literary work. "Watership Down" has been praised by critics and readers alike from all over the world and of all different ages. The novel also earned Adams the Carnegie Medal, an honor not bestowed upon any of his other works.

"Watership Down" is unique in the fact that the characters are rabbits, rather than people, but Adams gives the rabbits very human qualities and feelings. Though the story itself is obviously fictional, the geographical information in the novel is quite accurate. Adams based the environment the rabbits live in around the area he grew up in so the landmarks that are seen in the novel are true to life, and places that Adams has actually been. The novel gives the reader an insight into a world they would never usually think twice about. In mankind's tendency to destroy nature and never think twice, animals are losing their homes and being totally uprooted from everything they know, and in a lot of cases are killed. Adams has a knack for really personifying the rabbits, so the reader thinks of them as humans. He paints a picture of the importance of being a part of nature, rather than separating oneself from it.

Plot

"Watership Down" follows a group of rabbits in search of a new home (warren). Fiver, a very small rabbit, has a sixth sense and can tell when something either very bad or very good is going to happen. Fiver and his brother Hazel decide to leave and are joined by a handful of friends and other rabbits from the warren who believe Fiver. The rabbits eventually come across a nice field with plenty of food where they think they can settle down, despite the fact that there are other strange rabbits living there. Fiver tells the rabbits not to join this warren because he has a bad feeling and is proven right when one of the rabbits; Bigwig, gets caught in a trap, and they realize that the food is there to lure rabbits, so a farmer can trap them. The rabbits move on acquiring a new travel companion, a rabbit named Strawberry.

The rabbits come to a place called Watership Down where Fiver believes they should settle. Once the rabbits begin to settle in Hazel realizes that they have no does (female rabbits) and thus have no way of reproducing. Hazel sets out to find some does and encounters the evil General Woundwart, leader of the Efrafa warren, who is trapping rabbits. Hazel is badly injured, and thought to be dead, in his attempts to rescue the trapped rabbits. They continue to the nearby warren to find some does and formulate a plan to escape with them, though it is foiled by Captain Campion, General Woundwort's right-hand rabbit, who leads a large scale attack with his army. Hazel sets a farm dog on the attacking rabbits and is nearly eaten by a cat, but the rabbits get away accompanied by does and live happily in their warren at Watership Down where Hazel lives for several years, an impressive lifespan for a rabbit.

Characters

Hazel

Hazel is the leader of the rabbits who are looking for a new place to live, and also the brother of Fiver. Hazel is a very fair leader and is heroic in his actions. He is close with every member of the group and knows their strengths and uses each of them as they are fit. He puts himself in dangerous situations often to help his group and more than once has a brush with death. Hazel is a great thinker and is instrumental in formulating plans of action against other warrens who threaten them. Hazel is very loyal and brave; others are loyal to him, as well.

Fiver

Fiver is the runt of the group, and if it were not for this fact would probably be seen as the leader of the group; instead his brother, Hazel, takes over that role. Fiver is a seer and thus can tell when a dangerous situation is about to happen and the rabbits in his group trust in and rely on these instincts. In the original warren, the rabbits belonged to Fiver got the feeling that they should all move because disaster would strike and many members did not take him seriously so did not leave with Fiver and the others. Later we learn that Fiver's instincts were spot on because the warren had been poisoned and most rabbits did not survive.

Bigwig

Bigwig was one of the officers of the original warren. Despite the fact that other officers did not see any threat in Fiver's visions, Bigwig decided to trust in him and leave anyway. Bigwig is the strongest of the rabbits that became refugees and loves a good battle. Bigwig is very intelligent and is a good strategist that knows when it is appropriate to fight or when it is necessary to stand down. It is Bigwig's plan that eventually defeats General Woundwort, which shows that he is cunning as well as powerful and is capable of winning out over much stronger adversaries.

General Woundwort

The General is the main antagonist of the novel. He is the leader of the Efrafa warren and is shown to be a quite tyrannous leader. Woundwort was orphaned as a young rabbit, and grew to be massive, strong, vicious and savage. His strength can be compared to that of Bigwig, though he does not have any of Bigwig's compassion and kindness. Woundwort makes it his mission to destroy Hazel's warren and Watership Down, but he is not smart enough and eventually is defeated, almost killing his own warren in the process. After Bigwig dies, he becomes a rabbit legend known as the Bogeyman.

Captain Campion

Captain Campion is the General's best Captain, and what one may call his right-hand rabbit. Captain Campion leads an army in an attack against Watership Down, though is eventually shown to be quite brave and fair. He ends up leading the Efrafan warren back to their home and helps to set up a warren in between Efrafa and Watership Down with Hazel. Captain Campion's strongest skill is that he is a skilled tracker, which is probably why he was used to lead the Efrafan troops in their attack against the Down.

Captain Holly

Holly is the leader of the Sandleford warren and refuses to leave with Fiver, Hazel, and the others because he sees no threat in Fiver's visions. When Sandleford is destroyed, Holly is one of the survivors and meets up with Hazel's warren and wishes to become a part of their efforts. Hazel is at first wary of the possibility that Holly will make an attempt to upstage him but soon learns that Holly is okay with taking a lesser role than the one he had once taken. Holly proves to be a dedicated and hard-working addition to the group and brings his skills as a strong fighter and skilled tracker.

Blackberry

Blackberry is one of the refugee rabbits and the strength that he brings to the group is his intelligence. He is by far the most intelligent and astute member of the group which makes him Hazel's go-to rabbit for advice when creating a strategic plan. Blackberry has a knack for figuring things out that are truly puzzling to the other rabbits, and things that most of them do not even understand after Blackberry has figured them out. Blackberry is the brains of the operation, and the one Hazel goes to when he needs an idea.

Dandelion

Dandelion is also a member of Hazel's group, and his main contribution is his speed. Dandelion is the fasted of the rabbits and often is asked to go ahead of the other rabbits to scout because Hazel knows that Dandelion is so fast that he will not be caught if he comes into a bad situation. Dandelion is known to tell many stories to entertain the other rabbits, mainly stories of Eh-ahrairah. Dandelion is a very loyal member of the group and is a crucial part of keeping the rabbits safe because of his useful speed.

El-ahrairah

Though El-ahrairah is not technically a character in the book, he is mentioned often. He is the main character in every story that the rabbits tell one another, especially Dandelion. He is a courageous folk hero and the idol of many of the rabbits, especially Hazel who takes inspiration from El-ahrairah's heroism. Though El-ahrairah is fictional, he lays the guidelines, values, and rules for the rabbits, and they are happy to follow his lead. He seems to represent a God-like character in that the rabbit's worship of him and accordance to his values seems reminiscent of religion.

Blackavar

Blackavar was a member of the Efrafa warren but tried to escape and was caught. After he was caught, he was mutilated and hung on display to show the others rabbits the repercussions of their actions should they attempt to make an escape, as well. Blackavar is rescued by Bigwig and joins Hazel's group where he is accepted though not fully trusted until he proves his loyalty. He proves to be an expert tracker as well as a skilled ranger, which are useful qualities and welcome additions to the Watership Down warren.

Kehaar

Kehaar is not a rabbit at all but a black-headed gull that is injured. He rests in Watership Down and is treated in a friendly manner by Hazel and the other rabbits, thus becoming quite loyal to them. Kehaar is a strange character due to his unique accent and the interesting way he puts things into words. He is often impatient but is thankful for the rabbits regardless. Once his wing is fixed, Kehaar helps the rabbits to track down the Efrafa rabbits, and also acts as a diversion to give the Down rabbits a leg up on the competition. After he is fully recovered, Kehaar leaves the Down and returns to his own colony.

Clover

Hazel and his crew rescued Clover from the Nuthinger farm where she was being held. Clover was a domestic rabbit and had been raised in a cage; therefore, she was not accustomed to living in the wild. Despite the fact that she had been raised in captivity, she acclimated to wildlife easily. Clover mates with another rabbit, Speedwell and becomes pregnant. Clover is the very first doe in the new Watership Down warren to give birth to a litter of babies.

Strawberry

Strawberry is a member of the warren of the snares, or Cowslip's warren. While Hazel and the others are briefly staying with the warren of the snares, they befriend Strawberry, and he decides to leave with them when they move on. Strawberry is taken into the group without question, but it takes a while before he is fully trusted. Strawberry proves to be an excellent addition to the warren due to his knack for digging up information, and also his knowledge of building. He is not used to living in the wild as the others are, but he contributes in every way he can and proves himself quite useful.

Silver

Silver was a member of the Sandleford warren who was not going to leave when Fiver gave his warning, but Bigwig convinced him to. Silver is large and strong and a very skilled fighter who is an immense help in hostile situations. Silver is a very experienced rabbit and is able to grasp his surroundings and assess his situations quickly and accurately. Hazel often counts on Silver to be an asset to the group when presented with a confrontation and knows that Silver will always do what he sees best for the entire group, as his instincts are mostly correct.

Hyzenthlay

Hyzenthlay is another doe that was brought to Watership Down. She was a member of the Efrafan warren and is very strong, smart, and kind. When Bigwig sets loose the other Efrafan does Hyzenthlay helps him to do so and is appreciated for her efforts. She is somewhat of a seer, like Fiver, and thus proves a strong asset to the group. Once settled in Watership Down Hyzenthlay mates with Holly. Hyzenthlay and Holly are the parents to the second litter of rabbits born in the Down.

Themes

Home

This novel really expresses the notion that "home is where the heart is". To many people in the original warren they could not see moving somewhere away from their home, but to Fiver, Hazel, and the others, home would be wherever they decided to make it. There were a few places along the way that the rabbits considered calling their home, but they did not settle on one until they reached Watership Down. They are in a constant search for the best home they can make and are at times blinded by something that appears perfect on the surface, such as the farm with the traps and abundance of food.

Heroism

Hazel and Fiver can both be seen as heroic figures in this novel for different reasons. Fiver saves the rabbits by leading them away from the warren they had been living in, sensing correctly that something bad was about to happen. Hazel is a hero because, as the leader of the rabbits, he put himself in harm's way to ensure that the rest of the rabbits were safe. He risked his own life to rescue other rabbits from the traps, even those he did not have a friendship with. "Watership Down" tends to follow the same heroic path as the classic epic tales of past years.

Leadership

Every mission must have a leader and Hazel was the leader of this one. Hazel took his leadership role seriously by playing the hero and steering his troops in the right direction. He took the initiative in formulating plans and in launching counter-attacks against the other more sinister rabbits. Hazel did not count on others to do his dirty work for him; he did the rescuing and the fighting himself. Leadership is also seen in Captain Campion and General Woundwort, though in a less favorable light as someone always needs to be the bad guy in a hostile situation.

Chauvinism

Though it may not have been Adams' intention, the tale of "Watership Down" has a definite chauvinist air to it. The rabbits that are travelling together are all males, and go through a lot of experiences that could be considered as male bonding. After the rabbits find a place to live their entire goal, is to find female rabbits to mate with, which is true to life yet chauvinistic regardless. The men are the leaders, the fighters, and the heroes while the females are the baby-makers, a stereotype which humans have worked many years to put to rest.

Nature

An important theme of this novel is the ease of nature and living a natural life. Fiver, Hazel, and the other rabbits are not attracted to a life they deem to be unnatural or uneasy because they prefer the simple life of finding food and wandering free, rather than being confined. The other warrens that the rabbits come into contact with are unnatural to Fiver and Hazel because they live a life that is too controlled and inorganic, much like humans. Humans tend to live a life outside of nature, and with little or no regard to it, whereas to the rabbits a natural life is the only way to live.

Religious Symbolism

While Adams' maintains that there are no religious undertones to the novel, there is a bit of an argument to the contrary. Rabbits obviously will not identify with a specific religion or believe in a God, but they do tell their own stories of El-ahrairah, a hero amongst rabbits who has been a hero of rabbit legend for some time. El-ahrairah is a symbol for the rabbits to look up to and an example to follow. In a sense, he is their idol and gives them something to aspire to, which is what religion is for many people. In a way, he is their God and the figure they hold on a pedestal.

Idealism

There does seem to be a bit of a political leaning in the novel, in the description of the different societies mainly. The rabbits are in search of the ideal warren and Hazel aspires to be the ideal leader like his idol, El-ahrairah. One society they meet is like a brainwashed cult who are basically setting themselves up for the slaughter, and another society is a group of hostiles who are ready to declare war at the slightest intrusion from any rabbits outside their warren. Watership Down becomes the ideal warren that the rabbits are looking for with the idea democratic environment.

Tolerance

Staying with the concept of having the ideal society, the rabbits of Fiver and Hazel's warren are tolerant and accommodating of other animals. They go out of their way to befriend other animals, and help to find them food. The rabbits do befriend the other animals to serve their own purposes, but they do not discriminate against other animals because they are different as the rabbits from other warrens did. They were welcoming and friendly in every encounter until they were attacked, though none of the other warrens even made an attempt to socialize.

Friendship

The journey that Fiver and Hazel set out on began and ended with those they were close to. The friends of Fiver trusted his instincts that something bad was to happen and allowed him to steer them in the right direction. The comradery that is shared by the rabbits helps them to keep a clear head through the trials they face and forms the base of a strong environment and community. Hazel becomes the ideal leader because not only is he fair and helpful, but he is a friend to those who are following his lead, as a good leader should be.

Brains vs. Brawn

There are different levels of passivity within the novel, shown by the various warrens. The warren led by Captain Campion is passive-aggressive and act with little thought. They have a fighting mentality and do not seem to plan their moves much before they make them. The strange warren at the farm was filled with very passive rabbits. The rabbits did not make any moves to free themselves from what would surely be their demise, either in thought or in action. Hazel's warren were thinkers and doers. The members of the warren led by Hazel would strategize and formulate creative plans before they would act, which brought them success; the use of brainpower easily defeated the use of nothing but brawn.

Chapter Summaries

Chapters 1-10

At the opening of the novel, a group of young rabbits of the Sandleford warren are searching for food. Hazel and Fiver are both only a year old and have not yet reached their fully growth but it appears obvious that Hazel will be quite a large rabbit and Fiver is very small. Hazel and Buckthorn are hoping to find some cowslip to eat and Fiver finds it for them, but they are reprimanded by another rabbit named Toadflax who reminds them that cowslip is a delicacy reserved for the Owsla, the higher order of rabbits. Fiver, who possesses a form of rabbit ESP, gets a feeling that something bad is about to happen to their warren. He sees a sign that they cannot read, but knows it is related to the feeling he is having. He sees a field covered in blood, but Hazel tells him that he is just seeing the reflection of the sun. The sign reads that a housing development will soon be built right on top of their warren, though they have no idea.

During the night, Fiver has a nightmare about the warren being destroyed and wakes Hazel. Fiver tells Hazel that they must evacuate immediately and convince all of the other rabbits to leave with them. In the morning, Hazel takes Fiver to meet with the Chief rabbit, Threarah. He is guarded by the Owsla and on this day he is being guarded by Bigwig. Hazel convinces Bigwig to allow them to see the Chief, who listens tolerantly to Fiver's warnings, but tells them that he sees no threat, and they will stay, because it is safer for a warren to stay put than to travel. Hazel implores him to see differently because Fiver's visions have always been right before, but he refuses. After they leave, Hazel and Fiver hear the Threarah reprimanding Bigwig for allowing them to interrupt him.

Hazel and Fiver decide they will leave the warren anyway and find a few rabbits to join them. For rabbits that are not a part of the Owsla, life is grim and leaving seems better than staying with danger looming. The group is approached by Bigwig who has decided to leave the Owsla and tells Hazel that he thinks he can get some other Owsla members to join them as many of them are becoming discontented with the way they are treated. Hazel warns Bigwig to steer clear of Captain Holly, the head of the police and decides that the group will leave the warren that night.

Hazel and Fiver are joined by many others: Pipkin, Dandelion, Hawkbit, Blackberry, Buckthorn, Acorn, and Speedwell. When Bigwig arrives he is joined by Silver, another member of the Owsla who has just become a member but trusts Bigwig's decision. As they are about to leave they are approached by Captain Holly, who tries to arrest Bigwig and Silver. Holly believes that the rabbits are forming a committee to overthrow the Chief, which is obviously not their plan. Bigwig is much bigger and stronger than Holly and attacks him, and Hazel tells him that if he does not back off he will be killed. Holly leaves and the rabbits depart immediately for fear of death upon the return of the guards.

The rabbits begin on their journey, keeping a decent pace but remaining cautious of the unknown territory. Hazel takes it upon himself to lead the group and sometimes goes ahead to make sure the path they are on is safe. After a while, the smaller rabbits become very tired and Hazel decides they should all rest for the night. To keep the rabbits' spirits high, Hazel asks Dandelion to tell them a story, as he is known for. Dandelion tells of El-ahrairah, a rabbit that is a hero in folklore that is skillful, intelligent, and at times dishonest, but with the understanding that those he tricks will have every right to trick him back.

Dandelion tells the El-ahrairah story about the creation. Frith, the sun-god that is worshipped by rabbits, asks El-ahrairah to make his people stop reproducing because there are so many of them, but El-ahrairah refuses. Frith decides to trick El-ahrairah by telling him that he will be meeting with all of the animals separately to present them each with a gift, which El-ahrairah is very excited about. On his way, to see Frith he stops to rest and is told that Frith is giving the enemies of the rabbits' gifts that will help them to outsmart and kill the rabbits. El-ahrairah fears this and digs a hole to hide from Frith, but Frith catches up to him when he is halfway hanging out of the hole. Frith feels bad for El-ahrairah and blesses him with a fluffy tail and very strong hind legs to help him to escape when he is being hunted by others.

When the story reaches the end, the rabbits hear a lendri (badger) nearby. They are unsure as to whether the badger is harmful to them so upon Bigwig's suggestion they run quickly away from the spot they had been resting. They reach a river, and Fiver knows that they should cross the river, but they do not know how to do that, especially because of how tired a couple of the rabbits are. Bigwig gets a bit snippy with Hazel, but Hazel, demonstrating his leadership skills, merely thanks Bigwig for helping them to escape. Bigwig tells Hazel that the badger is more of a threat to small rabbits, but not so much the adults. They see a field on the other side of the river that looks favorable to the woods they have been traveling but are stuck.

The rabbits sit and think about how to get across the river, whether they should walk further upstream or cross there. Hazel sends Bigwig across the water to scout out the situation, and he returns with the news that they must cross there because there is a dog roaming the woods, and it will be dangerous for them. Pipkin and Fiver are too small, and tired to swim across on their own, so the rabbits think of a way to get across. Blackberry sees a plank of wood and suggests floating them across on the wood, though the other rabbits do not understand what he means. Bigwig understands and helps Blackberry and eventually the rabbits all make it across, though most of them are still confused about what has just happened.

While the other rabbits are sleeping Hazel takes off to find a safer place for them to rest, fearing that they will be targeted out in the open. He finds a place with plants he does not recognize that will shield them from predators. Bigwig and Silver recognize them as bean plants and know that the smell will keep them safe, as well. However, a crow zeroes in on Fiver and Pipkin and goes in for the attack. Bigwig and Silver scare the crow off, telling the rest of the group that crows are cowards and only attack those they see as weak. The rabbits set in to rest, and Hazel removes the thorn that Pipkin had gotten lodged into his paw. Still uneasy about their safety, Hazel stays up to watch out for predators.

The rabbits hear a gunshot that wakes them in the morning and decide to hurry on their way. They reach a road and see a car going by, but are confused because they know nothing about roads. Bigwig explains that the cars are only dangerous at night because their bright lights paralyze rabbits, so they often get hit. Hazel leads everyone across the road and is approached by Speedwell, Acorn, and Hawkbit who tell him that they do not believe Fiver and want to go back, which Hazel tells them is ridiculous. Bigwig reprimands them for entertaining such a notion and Fiver asks to talk to Hazel. Fiver seems to be in a trance and tells Hazel that though they will face danger they must make it to some hills in the distance. When Fiver comes to he does not remember what he said to Hazel and Hazel seems worried about the distance they must travel to reach the hills.

Chapters 11-20

Acorn, Hawkbit, and Speedwell confronted Bigwig, asking who the real chief was, him or Hazel. In response, Bigwig bit Hawkbit. Hazel knows the rabbits are not happy and are worried that the mission is fruitless, and he promises them that he will get them somewhere safe where they can settle down. The next morning Hazel leads the rabbits to a large field full of tall grass that the rabbits are very happy about. Blackberry tells Hazel that he is truly their Chief and although Acorn, Hawkbit, and Speedwell are obviously still bitter they enjoy the grass with the other rabbits.

In the field, the rabbits begin to dig holes to shelter themselves from the rain that will be coming, though digging is unfamiliar work to them because usually the does are the ones who do the digging in the warrens. The rabbits are visited by another rabbit that is very large and has very nice fur. The rabbit's name is Cowslip, and he tells the rabbits they are welcome to join his warren as there are plenty of burrows for all of them, noticing that the holes they have dug are quite shallow. They tell him that they would like to talk it over, and he leaves as the rain comes. Fiver does not think it is a good idea because he senses something bad will happen, but the other rabbits, including Hazel, decide to give it a shot.

The rabbits head to Cowslip's warren and meet a rabbit named Strawberry who befriends Hazel and begins to show him around. The only rabbit who does not make himself at home is Fiver, who stays in the shadows. The rabbits see many empty burrows and are invited to settle into any that they wish as there are plenty to spare. Hazel notices that there are many strange structures around and finds that Strawberry, suspiciously, changes the subject anytime he is asked a question about the origins of something.

Blackberry, Pipkin, and Hazel tell Cowslip that they want to eat outside in the rain, and so he laughs at them, which they find strange because they do not understand laughter. Once outside the rabbits feel free to discuss how strange this new warren is though they seem nice enough. In the morning, Strawberry wakes the rabbits to tell them that the rain has ended, and the man who lives close has thrown some food out for them. They find carrots and other food scraps in the field, which they eat, and bring the rest back to the burrow with them. Fiver does not join in the feasting and refuses to even go into the burrow because he feels like something is very wrong with the situation. Finally, convincing Fiver to come with them that they reenter the burrow and tell the other rabbits a story about El-ahrairah, as they did not seem interested to hear the tales of the Sandleford warren.

In the story, El-ahrairah has been sentenced to live in the marshes forever because of the torment he has bestowed upon other animals. He asks Prince Rainbow, a prophet of Frith, if he can be allowed out of the marsh if he can bring all of the King's lettuce to him. El-ahrairah and another rabbit called Rabscuttle convince the kingdom that the lettuce heads are tainted and will make everyone sick. The King decides to send the lettuce to the marsh to kill the rabbits, which of course is what El-ahrairah wanted because the lettuce was not tainted at all. Prince Rainbow has no choice but to allow El-ahrairah out of the marsh, and as the story goes, from that moment on rabbits could never be kept from a vegetable garden.

Hazel and others feel that the new rabbits must be very accepting of them now that Dandelion has told such a classic rabbit story to them, but they seem disturbed because they feel rabbits should not have to rely on trickery, but have dignity. One of the rabbits by the name of Silverweed recites a poem he has written about life and the poem causes Fiver to act very strangely and cry out in agony. The other rabbits bring Fiver outside, and he is relieved that they finally seem to be listening to his warnings, though he is surprised to learn that his is not the case at all, they are upset with him for possibly ruining their relationship with the new warren.

When Hazel awakes the next day he realizes that Fiver is not there. He and Bigwig catch up with Fiver, and he tells them that he is leaving. Bigwig accuses Fiver of causing a scene just so others will follow him and turns to walk away but gets caught in a snare. Fiver comes back with the help for Bigwig, and they get him out of the snare. When Bigwig realizes that the rabbits from Cowslip's warren would not come to help, he declares that he will go kill them, and some other rabbits agree. Fiver stops them, sharing with them what he has surmised from their experiences: the farmer that puts food out for them is really trapping them and the other rabbits know this but ignore the fact and live in their own little world to pass the time. They decide they must leave immediately and are joined by Strawberry who wishes to go with them.

Over the next day, the rabbits travel three miles, glad to have survived their time with Cowslip's warren and immensely trusting of one another and Fiver's instincts after their ordeal. They take some time to rest in a barn but leave soon after being attacked by rats which are fought off by Silver, Buckthorn, and Bigwig. The rabbits finally arrive at the downs, but Fiver still wants them to climb to the top, which is where he knows they should be. Hazel, Dandelion, and Hawkbit climb to the top and report back that it seems the perfect place for them, and there are plenty of burrow holes on the way up for the group to stop and rest.

The rabbits have a good night's sleep, happy that they have reached their destination. The next day the rabbits decide to build a warren, which is usually a job for does, but since they do not have any does they do it themselves. Hazel, Speedwell, Bigwig, and Dandelion decide to go down the hill a bit to find some grass and hear a voice calling out Bigwig's name and making a terrible sound. They find that the voice belongs to Captain Holly who looks to be in terrible condition, as though he may keel over at any moment. He is accompanied by Bluebell and seems to be very scared.

Back at the warren, Strawberry is teaching the other rabbits how to build a honeycomb structure in the roots of the trees to live in, which gives them a lot of space. Hazel helps a mouse without really meaning to but it gives him the idea to help other animals so that the animals may help them when they need it, as well. The other rabbits think that Hazel is completely nuts for wanting to help other animals and Bigwig wonders if soon their warren will be swarming with other animals. The mouse feels indebted to Hazel and the other rabbits for helping him and promises to return the favor.

Chapters 21-30

Holly tells the other rabbits that he has no intentions
of taking over the leadership role in their warren; he
is simply looking for a safe place and would like to
stay with them. He tells the story of what happened
back at the Sandleford warren, which he is horrified
by. A group of men came, one of them carrying a
gun, and put poisonous gas in the open rabbit holes,
trapping and killing most of the warren. The only
rabbits that escaped were Holly, Bluebell, and another
rabbit named Pimpernel. They followed Hazel's trail
and came upon Cowslip's warren, which attacked
them and killed Pimpernel who was already weak.
Hazel almost killed Cowslip but left him alone after
he told them where Hazel and the others had gone.

Hazel tells the group why he saved the mouse. He feels that it will be helpful to makes friends with animals that they have common enemies with. Hawkbit tells the rabbits of a place where they can eat really good grass that a mouse told him about earlier. Hazel is excited that saving the other mouse had paid off in this way. Bluebell tells the rabbits another El-ahrairah story that took place shortly after the story about the King's lettuce. Prince Rainbow wanted to punish El-ahrairah and Rabscuttle for their trickery, so he made a rabbit named Hufsa live with El-ahrairah, and sent Rabscuttle to live elsewhere. Hufsa was a nark, so El-ahrairah made him look like an idiot, and put him through many strange situations so that when he tried to tell the story of what had happened no one would believe him, and it worked.

Hazel finds a black-headed gull that has an injured wing and tries to convince the bird that they would like to help it, though the bird does not seem to want their help. Hazel is relentless and tells the bird, named Kehaar, that they will build it a hole and nurse him back to health. The bird begins to feel better and is more receptive to the rabbits, becoming friends with Bigwig. Hazel has a plan to use the bird to fly off and find them some does because without does their warren is fruitless. When Kehaar gets better he goes on a mission to find does and returns with the news that there are some does on a farm at the bottom of the hill and another warren not too far off. The next day Strawberry, Silver, Buckthorn, and Holly take off to find the other warren.

Hazel decides that while the other rabbits are looking for the other warren he and Pipkin will travel to the farm and find some does for them. He finds rabbits living in hutches on the farm and goes to talk to them. He finds that there are two bucks and two does, and he asks them if they would like to join his warren, promising to come back and free them later. A cat appears, and Hazel gets the cat to lunge at them, and they narrowly escape it. Pipkin questions why Hazel wished to speak to the other rabbits and Hazel tells him that he will explain it to him later.

When Hazel and Pipkin return to the warren Fiver is upset that Hazel went to find does, believing that he is trying to upstage Holly, who will undoubtedly return with some does of his own. Hazel plans an expedition to free the rabbits from the hutches, being sure to bring Blackberry with him to figure out how to open the latches. Fiver senses that they should not go to the farm because something bad will happen and Hazel promises not to go onto the farm alone. The rabbits attack a cat on the farm and release the rabbits from the hutches. Men pull up in a car to stop the rabbits from leaving, and one of them shoots Hazel. The other rabbits see blood and go back to the warren to tell Fiver what happened, though Fiver has already seen it in a vision. Soon Silver, Strawberry, Holly, and Buckthorn return, with no does, and all are injured with the exception of Silver.

Fiver has a dream that night that Hazel is still alive and when he wakes he asks Blackberry to take him to the spot where Hazel was shot, though Blackberry is convinced that Hazel cannot possibly be alive. Fiver sees the trail of blood on the farm and follows it to a drain where he finds Hazel, miraculously still alive.

The rabbits back at the warren do not know what to do without Hazel and Holly tells the story of what happened when they met the Efrafa warren. They were confronted by three large rabbits and brought into the warren, discovering that they lived in a very strict environment with many rules and regulations. They were brought before a council to tell General Woundwort and Captain Campion why they were there. They learned a lot about the rabbits, befriending a doe named Hyzenthlay. It did not take long before they realized that they were prisoners, rather than guests. When they finally escaped they got home only to realize that Hazel had been killed in the barn raid.

Blackberry comes into the warren and tells everyone that Hazel is alive and at the bottom of the hill with a shotgun wound. Bigwig goes down to see Hazel and finds that he is sleeping. The next day Kehaar arrives and helps to remove the pellets from Hazel's leg. Hazel rests for a few days, but still leads the group in what he wishes them to do. He instructs them to return to Efrafa to find some does, asking Blackberry to help formulate a foolproof plan.

Hazel returns to the warren the next morning, mostly healed and tells the other rabbits that he will be going to Efrafa to find some does. Holly believes that it will be a suicide mission, but Hazel assures him that there is a good plan in place, and Fiver even agrees, believing that it will work. Blackberry jumps on board, as do Silver, Pipkin, and Kehaar. Kehaar states that he will help them to find some does but must return to his colony immediately after that, promising that he will return to visit them soon. The rabbits set out with only Holly, Strawberry, Buckthorn, and the hutch rabbits staying behind. Kehaar lets the rabbits know that they will be safe hiding on the other side of the river and when they are settled Hazel asks Dandelion to tell an El-ahrairah story.

Chapter 31-40

The El-ahrairah story was about the time he tried to get rid of King Darzin for once and for all. He and Rabscuttle sought out the Black Rabbit, the rabbit that Frith appointed to determine when each rabbit would die, to offer a trade of his life for those of the rest of the rabbits that King Darzin would not leave alone. The Black Rabbit did not want anything to do with El-ahrairah and so El-ahrairah tried some of his trickery on him, losing him whiskers, ears, and tale in the process. The Black Rabbit told El-ahrairah that King Darzin's soldiers were already taken care of, and when El-ahrairah and Rabscuttle returned home they saw that all the rabbits were happy and at peace and the warren was thriving. Frith arrived to return the things El-ahrairah had lost and to explain to him that wisdom does not come easily. Pipkin interrupted the story time to tell the rabbits that a fox was near them.

Hazel tells all of the rabbits to run from the fox, but Bigwig runs toward it. He disappears into the bushes, and Hazel hears a rabbit squeal and sees Bigwig run back out. Bigwig explains that, he ran, into three strange rabbits in the bush and told them to run, but they resisted and tried to stop him , so Bigwig knocked one down, and assumed that the squeal must have been the rabbit getting attacked by the fox. The rabbits keep moving, and Kehaar tells them that there is a patrol ahead that will find them if they do not take cover soon. The rabbits cross the railroad tracks where Kehaar tells them that they are safe and find a place to rest for the night.

Hazel thinks that the rabbits that Bigwig encountered were probably members of a patrol that were close to finding them and it is a good thing he broke them up. Kehaar leads the rabbits to the river and shows them a bridge to cross, though the rabbits are quite reluctant even though Fiver tells them that the bridge is fine. After crossing the river, the rabbits find a place to rest, and figure out a plan. They come to another river with a smaller bridge and happen upon a boat that Blackberry decides they should use for themselves. Hazel tells Bigwig that it is time for him to go ahead, and somewhat reluctantly he heads out.

General Woundwort, the leader of the Efrafa rabbits, is a fearless fighter who has battled many enemies. He created the Efrafa because he wanted to feel powerful and has maintained complete control over them from the beginning. The patrols the rabbits take turns with are a way of keeping the Efrafa safe from outsiders. The Efrafa have been weakened by Hazel's warren due to the death of one of their officers when Holly and the others escaped, and also the fox attack. Captain Campion comes to Woundwort and tells him that a rabbit has come who wishes to become a part of the Efrafa. The rabbit is Bigwig, and Woundwort does not know he is in alliance with Holly, so he does not foresee a threat and makes Bigwig an officer.

With Bigwig's new job, he begins to learn about the security measures of the Efrafa rabbits. He discovers that their security is tight and thinks that breaking some of the rabbits out will be harder than he anticipated. He makes friends with a rabbit named Blackavar who wishes to leave Efrafa. He tried to leave once but was caught, mutilated, and put on display to be an example for other rabbits thinking of leaving. Bigwig also meets Hyzenthlay, a very intelligent doe, and tells her his plan to break some of them free. Hyzenthlay wishes to help Bigwig and go with him, telling him that they must make their move in the next couple of days while her mark is still allowed outside, or they will not have a chance.

Bigwig is woken by one of the officers because it is time for his Mark to go feed. While eating, he sees Kehaar; he passes the message that the other rabbits must be ready at sunset and that Kehaar will have to be ready to attack if needed. Bigwig finds Hyzenthlay and her friend and tells them of the plan. Just when he is about to leave that night Bigwig is called aside by Woundwort to talk.

Woundwort tells Bigwig that he is concerned because a member of his guard recognizes Bigwig from the fox encounter. Bigwig explains that he did not mean for the fox to attack the other rabbits, and did not know anything about the other rabbits that had been near, he had only seen their tracks. Woundwort invites Bigwig on a guard a few days later and asks him to watch out for Hyzenthlay because he believes there may be trouble where she is concerned. Hazel and the others worry when Bigwig does not appear as he said, knowing that something must have gone wrong with the plan. Bigwig worries that too many does know the plan, and they will be caught, but nonetheless tells them, and Blackavar to be ready that night. He also manages to get word to Kehaar of the change in plan.

Kehaar gets the message to Hazel, and others and they prepare themselves for what is to come. In the middle of the night, Bigwig is wakened by Hyzenthlay who informs him that one of the does has been arrested and Bigwig knows that it is time to go because obviously Woundwort is catching on. Bigwig frees Blackavar, attacking his guards, and the rabbits make a break for it together. Woundwort notices the rabbits escaping and Bigwig knows it will not be long before they are chased. Just as Woundwort and Campion caught up and were about to attack lightning struck and Kehaar and the other rabbits came out of nowhere to rescue Bigwig and the others.

The rabbits float downriver discussing what to do next when they come to a bridge that Kehaar does not think they will fit under. They do fit, though one of the does that has escaped from Efrafa with them is injured in the process. At the next bridge, the boat gets stuck, and Kehaar tells the rabbits they will have to jump off the boat and swim under the bridge, though the rabbits are quite skeptical of this advice. Hazel, Pipkin, and Blackavar take it upon themselves to jump first, and find it is safe; they make their way to the bank, telling the other rabbits to do the same. Eventually all of the rabbits make it ashore and stop to sleep.

The rabbits awaken in the morning, preparing to continue on to the down, and realize that the doe who had been hurt while passing under the bridge has died in the night. Sad as they are, the rabbits know that they must move on. Kehaar leaves the rabbits to return to his colony but promises that he will rejoin them once the winter has ended. Blackavar uses his training from Efrafa to track for the group, proving himself a useful addition. The rabbits come upon a place Hazel, and Fiver feel will be good to dig holes to rest in for a few days. Blackavar is skeptical because he feels they are in fox country, but they stay anyway. A few days later Blackavar's instincts prove correct because one of the does is taken by a fox. The rabbits encounter Captain Campion and his patrol along their way, but he does not challenge them because he is outnumbered. Blackavar insists that they must be killed, or they will report back to the Efrafans, but Hazel decides they will move on without violence. Campion follows them home and immediately heads back to Efrafa to tell Woundwort about the Down.

Chapter 41-Epilogue

When the rabbits settle in to the warren they find themselves to be quite content despite the fact that there are more bucks than does. Life is good for the rabbits, and they are eager to return to a normal rabbit life. Dandelion decides to tell the rabbits a story about EL-ahrairah. El-ahrairah and Rabscuttle decided to play a trick on a dog that was especially vicious because they wanted to get some good food, as was their usual motivation. They made the dog feel threatened and managed to make off with some delicious food while leaving the dog feeling as though he had saved his people from evil, so it was a win-win situation.

Hazel's friend the mouse visits and tells Hazel that he sees a group of rabbits nearing. Bigwig ignores the mouse, but Hazel feels as though it may be a threat, so he sends Holly and Blackavar to check out the situation. While they are gone, Speedwell reports to Hazel that Clover has given birth to the first litter of the warren. The rabbits return with the news that the Efrafa are coming and that General Woundwort is quite possibly with them, as well as Captain Campion. Hazel decides they must fill in all of the holes that lead to them, except for one so they can come and go and he leaves Bigwig in charge while he is gone.

Woundwort is determined to get revenge on Bigwig for the breakout because it undermined his authority and made the other rabbits less subservient to him. He decides to wait for them for the fox attack had happened, knowing that he would see them eventually. Hazel comes to Woundwort and offers to build a warren between the Down and Efrafa where rabbits, from both warrens can go to live, but Woundwort will not even entertain the notion. He tells Hazel that if all of the does, along with Bigwig and Blackavar do not come forward then he and his patrol will kill all of the bucks in Hazel's warren.

As the Efrafan, rabbits try to get into the warren Bigwig tells Hazel that all of the rabbits should hide in the burrows behind the honeycomb and block themselves in, and he will fight off Woundwort, who likely will not be able to get passed him and if so, not quickly. Fiver slips into one of his trances and Hazel gets an idea at the same exact time – he must get the dog from the farm. Hazel's idea came from an El-ahrairah story and he, Blackberry, and Dandelion head out to get the dog right away.

The three rabbits get to the farm and Blackberry stays back as lookout. Hazel chews on the leash that holds the dog while Dandelion guards him. The cat that had attacked the last time they were at the farm appears and lunges, which causes the dog to lunge back and break free from his leash. In all of the commotion Hazel falls from the kennel and notices the cat standing over him, staring.

Back at the warren Bigwig and others have covered all of the entrances except for one. Bigwig had to leave Fiver outside because he could not wake him from his trance, but Woundwort does not attack Fiver because he assumes he is already dead. When Woundwort and his patrol break through the newly made wall Bigwig attacks immediately, biting Woundwort in the leg. Woundwort lunges at Bigwig and is just about to go in for the kill when the wound on his leg causes it to give out, and Bigwig takes advantage.

On the farm, Dandelion gets the dog to chase after him toward Blackberry and the two rabbits together lead the dog toward the warren. Back at the warren Woundwort is having a hard time overtaking Bigwig, and Bigwig knows that even if Woundwort kills him, he will have trouble moving the body to get through the other rabbits that are hiding. Woundwort retreats to find a new way, telling one of his rabbits to go and fight Bigwig, but he is too scared. When they get above ground, they are greeted by Campion who tells them to all run because the dog is coming. Woundwort stands his grounds and tries to convince the rest of the rabbits to stand with him.

Back on the farm Hazel is rescued by Lucy, the little girl who lives on the farm. She hears Hazel screeching and rescues him from the cat, bringing him to see the doctor. The dog comes back to the farm at the same time Lucy finds Hazel, slightly wounded from his confrontation with Woundwort. The doctor tells Lucy that Hazel will be fine and brings her someplace to set him loose, which just happens to be at the base of the Down.

Back at the warren Hazel's group is victorious. When Woundwort was fighting against the dog his troops escaped with the aid of Captain Campion, and most of them managed to make it back to Efrafa alive. Some of the rabbits dove into the hole to avoid the dog, and there they met Fiver, who was up and alert; they immediately surrendered to him. Bigwig has managed to survive his ordeal, though he is quite hurt and all of the rabbits are excited to hear about Hazel's adventure on the farm.

By that October Watership Down is thriving and two more of the does have given birth to litters of kittens. The members of Efrafa that surrendered to Fiver surprisingly became members of the warren where they get along well with the rest of the rabbits, though they still fear that General Woundwart is alive somewhere and may not be done with his tyrannical rampage. Hazel still wishes to build a new warren between Watership Down and Efrafa, so the rabbits can feel free to mingle amongst others, and to quench the sense of adventure that the baby rabbits are developing, thanks to Bigwig who teaches them how to fight against cats.

A few years later the rabbits of the Down and the Efrafa rabbits are good friends and the third warren is up and running. The rabbits are all very happy, especially Hazel for what he had accomplished, and no one ever heard from Woundwort again though he did became a scary legend to tell future rabbits. Hazel has lived a much longer life than many rabbits do and one day he is approached by a rabbit, with light shining from his ears. The other rabbit asks Hazel to come with him and he does, happily, leaving his body behind him.

About BookCaps

We all need refreshers every now and then. Whether you are a student trying to cram for that big final, or someone just trying to understand a book more, BookCaps can help. We are a small, but growing company, and are adding titles every month.

Visit www.bookcaps.com to see more of our books, or contact us with any questions.

24519985R00031

Made in the USA
Lexington, KY
21 July 2013